Payback is a Witch

Rowland Bercy Jr.

Payback is a Witch

ISBN: 9781657352094

Payback is a Witch

ACKNOWLEDGMENTS

Thank you Rowland Bercy Sr.

Thank you Raquel Bercy

Thank you Shawn Scott

Thank you Chiara Noemi Monaco

Payback is a Witch

Prologue

Gwendolyn Boudreaux was a stunning woman of mixed heritage with warm mocha skin, olive-colored eyes, and hair black as bayou waters, which hung in loose dreads midway down her back. She was born and raised in New Orleans, Louisiana, the only child of immigrant travelers who migrated from France to Louisiana via Haiti. At the age of ten, Gwendolyn lost both of her parents, and with no other family to turn to, she soon found herself a ward of the state. For years, she was shuffled from one deplorable foster home to the next until she was eventually adopted by a stern but kind woman by the name of Louise Demerella, Who ran a small, elite boarding school for girls and welcomed Gwendolyn into her home and school with open arms.

Happy to be out of the foster care system, Gwendolyn seamlessly acclimated to her new environment and soon learned that both Louise and the school were not as they seemed to be. Shortly after her induction to her new home, Gwendolyn learned that Louise was, in actuality, the High Priestess of a small coven of inexperienced witches, which masqueraded as a boarding school. As High Priestess, Louise was charged with scrying for and recruiting budding young witches in an attempt to groom them to their full potential. Gwendolyn also discovered that she herself was a mystery as yet unrevealed. She learned that she was what some would call a natural witch, who was gifted at birth with an inborn ability to call upon and control the natural and super-natural powers of the universe—which she inherited from formidable and influential bloodlines, with each generation growing stronger than the last. Gwendolyn readily accepted Louise's revelation of her heritage, and with guidance from Louise, as well as her peers; she quickly learned to harness and command the energy present in all living things as well as the four elemental energies of earth, air, water, and fire.

Powerful she was indeed, and she committed herself whole-heartedly to her study of the craft, moving up in rank within the hierarchy of her coven expeditiously. By the age of twenty-five, Gwendolyn's thirst for knowledge outgrew the experience her coven was able to impart upon her, and without hesitation, she effortlessly transitioned from natural witch to contract witch, using esoteric tomes to summon forth denizens from unearthly realms to obtain knowledge, and thereby tremendously enhance her spell-casting abilities. While this practice was not frowned upon since spell craft is in every respect individualistic, it also was not highly publicized or widely practiced. Because of this, Gwendolyn voluntarily chose to exile herself from her coven and relocated to the more secluded wilderness of Slidell, on the Northeastern shore of Lake Pontchartrain, using the money she saved from clients seeking *"magical"* assistance to have a modest home built deep in the marshland, away from prying eyes where she could continue her studies uninterrupted.

Years passed, and by the age of thirty, Gwendolyn's spell-casting abilities grew, as did her reputation. People knew well the tale of the witch of the woods. Most thought the legend of a witch living deep in the swamp was nonsense, but in direct opposition, some believers would come from miles away and pay handsomely for her assistance—a love spell for this one, a spell seeking fortune for that one, a spell to exact revenge for another.

One sweltering summer's morning, a handsome broad-shouldered man paid Gwendolyn a visit. He had a rich mahogany complexion with strong facial features, high cheekbones, deep-set eyes that held a mischievous glint, and full lips containing what seemed to be a permanent smirk, as if he was recalling a funny story and on the verge of laughing aloud.

Instantly captivated with the robust stranger who had come in search of her assistance and lonely from her years of self-isolation, Gwendolyn invited the man into her home and with the help of a rather basic Charm Person spell, and her Goddess-given natural feminine wiles, Gwendolyn seduced and bedded her visitor. Their intercourse was intense and filled with fervor, and soon thereafter, both were exhausted from the magically encouraged tryst. After the conclusion of their lovemaking, Gwendolyn offered her visitor a beverage laced with just the right dose of Belladonna, lulling him into a deep slumber, which she knew would last at least a solid twelve hours.

Once he was fast asleep, Gwendolyn retrieved a small silver ring adorned with two sparkling green emeralds, which she secreted away in a hidden room that was built into the cottage upon its construction, wherein was kept all the components she used in her craft, along with her grimoire, which had become clunky and cumbersome with the many spells, rituals, and incantations she acquired over her years of study. In fact, her sacred book had become so burdensome that Gwendolyn invented a new and improved way of remembering, easily accessing, and transporting useful enchantments. With a little brainstorming, she eventually settled on creating what she termed 'casting-cards', each card serving as a quick reference resource and contained a visual representation of her spells and incantations, along with the necessary components needed for casting.

In addition to adopting a more convenient way of easily cataloging her enchatments, Gwendolyn also devised a rather fashion-forward method of having the components necessary for casting a desired spell readily available. Over her years of isolation, she discovered that she had a passion for and a talent at creating stunningly unique accessories within which she would meticulously incorporate multiple components needed for casting. So long as the necessary components for a particular spell were on her person when the words of the spell were spoken, the casting would be successful. Her daily routine would be to accessorize herself in one or more of her unique creations, assuring that she would have the necessary materials readily available if needed. For any spells demanding a combination of multiple components, Gwendolyn would prepare these in advance and tote them with her as required.

Gwendolyn located and read over the memory erase casting-card, knelt naked on the floor next to the cot her visitor rested quietly upon, and slipped the emerald ring onto her finger. She touched the ringed finger to her forehead and wiped the other hand back and forth through the air as if erasing writing from a chalkboard, she then chanted a mantra, weaving a spell of forgetfulness over her sleeping companion.

Casting such a high-level spell took every bit of concentration she could muster, and after eight hours, Gwendolyn slumped over on the floor, exhausted. She laid there for another hour recovering until she was able-bodied enough to rouse herself. When she finally had the energy to do so, Gwendolyn feebly dressed herself as well as her lover, who would not recall a single detail of their sexual escapade upon awaking, she then exited the cottage and waited. Sat in the evening sun, she allowed its warmth to refuel her depleted energies. It was well after dark by the time her visitor finally emerged from within.

"Ah, you're finally awake," Gwendolyn said, smiling.

"What happened?" the man asked, rubbing the back of his head in confusion.

"You passed out," Gwendolyn replied, "most likely a result of heat exhaustion. I figured you needed some time to recuperate so I allowed you to rest for a while."

The man stood silhouetted in the doorway of the cottage and stared sheepishly, eyes squinting, in an attempt to adjust to the night, "I'm sorry, I'm so embarrassed. I must have been out for hours. Hope I didn't cause you any trouble."

"Don't be silly, I was more than happy to watch over you while you rested," Gwendolyn offered in return, then added, "additionally, your sleep allowed me some time to arrange the assistance you came in search of," she continued, motioning to a box on a table next to the door. "Inside, you'll find all the items you need along with detailed instructions. Follow what I have written to the letter and, before you know it, the girl that you've set your sights on will fall head over heels in love with you."

The man looked perplexed, "but how did you know…" he started to ask.

Gwendolyn interrupted him with a sly grin and a wink, and said, "I wouldn't be much of a witch if I didn't know why you sought me out now, would I?"

Payback is a Witch

Of course, the stranger had told Gwendolyn the reason for his visit prior to the last twelve hours of his memory being erased, but she decided to keep that bit of information to herself for reputation's sake. The man looked puzzled and decided that pursuing the matter further was pointless. He then reached into his wallet, pulled out a wad of bills, and respectfully offered them to Gwendolyn.

"Damn that was easy, so how much do I owe you?" he asked, "and what happens if this doesn't work?"

Gwendolyn finally rose from the chair she was sitting in, walked over to the man, and gently refused his payment. "Keep your money, this one is on the house. Return home and if in two weeks' time your girl isn't drooling over you and begging you to marry her, come back and see me, it's not like I can up and move away." Gwendolyn said with a smile.

Payback is a Witch

The man started to protest but could see from the look in her eyes that the subject matter was not up for debate.

"Thank you so much," said Gwendolyn's handsome visitor, shaking her hand vigorously and staring at her with a sense of awe and wonder in his eyes. He picked up the box of supplies Gwendolyn prepared for him and began his journey home, barely able to believe his good fortune.

"Blessed be," Gwendolyn said with a smile on her face as he turned and walked away.

Gwendolyn watched her satisfied but unaware donor until he was obscured from view, swallowed up by a grove of massive cypress trees. She knew without a doubt that her days of loneliness would soon be behind her. Nine months later, Gwendolyn gave birth to a beautiful baby girl and the two lived in blissful isolation with Gwendolyn passing down the knowledge she acquired over the years to her very eager protégé.

Payback is a Witch

<u>1</u>

All Gwendolyn could do was watch with venom in her eyes as the five men viscously assaulted her daughter. The attack had been going on unabated for the past ten minutes with the men unscrupulously molesting and tormenting the girl. The thugs must have spotted Raven while she was in town and trailed her back from the city into the dense bayou, where they could have their way with her without interruption.

Once every few months, mother and daughter would make the six-mile hike from their home base to the city to collect any necessary supplies they might need, with Gwendolyn always halting a couple of miles before reaching the main road, at which point Raven would continue into town alone. Gwendolyn would then patiently await her daughter's return whereupon they would follow the same path back to the small cottage in which Raven and her mother continued to reside since Raven's birth some eighteen years ago. The two had made the trip to town countless times over the years without incident, until now.

"What do we have here, boys?" asked Charles, the obvious leader of the group. The man looked to be in his late twenties and was fairly good looking. He sported a classic crew cut and wore a pair of denim jeans with a black t-shirt, sporting a Siouxsie and the Banshees logo. Charles was standing behind Raven with one of his arms wrapped around her waist, pinning her arms to her side while his other hand savagely clawed at the front of her dress and pulled it down, ripping the front of her garment and exposing Raven's breasts to the marshland heat. Raven screamed and tried in vain to break free of Charles's unwanted embrace.

"Holy shit. Check out the tits on

this bitch," said Charles's younger brother, Brian, with a licentious look in his eye. Brian was shorter than his older brother, had a lean swimmer's build and rocked an edgy Faux Hawk. Brian stepped up and roughly grabbed a handful of Raven's swaying breasts and gave them a tight squeeze.

"I swear to Goddess you'll regret it if you don't get your filthy fucking hand off of me right now," spat Raven at the men. She was almost successful with landing a kick to Brian's crotch but he quickly sidestepped the blow.

"Oh, we've got a live one here," Brian taunted and then backhanded Raven across the face, splitting her lip in the process. He let go of her breasts and snatched a handful of her hair, yanking her head back and whispered menacingly in her ear, "that's it, fight back, bitch… that shit turns me the fuck on." Brian left a wet trail of spit down the side of Raven's face as he licked his way down her cheek and started biting and kissing her on the neck.

Ryan, Marcus, and Jason—the other members of the crew—stood by looking on with anticipation, anxiously awaiting their chance to have some fun with Raven.

"Get off me," Raven said. "I'm warning you."

"Just what are you going to do if we don't stop?" asked Charles. "Cast a spell on us?"

All the men laughed aloud at the implication. "Yeah, everyone knows what you and your hag of a mother claim to be. It is all a bunch of bullshit if you ask me. Witches are supposed to be ugly with green skin and warts. Yo fine ass definitely ain't any of those things. Now, your skank of a mother, she could possibly be a witch." Once again, all the men let out a roar of laughter. Charles violently threw Raven to the ground and all five men savagely set upon her.

Raven's screams brought no salvation.

2

Both women were, without question, formidable witches but Raven was still inexperienced and unable to do much in the way of fending off her attackers. Gwendolyn knew that any spell powerful enough to permanently dispatch all five of the men attacking her daughter would not be possible to cast successfully given the fact that most spells require considerable concentration and spoken word in addition to sometimes requiring material components, as well as measured and precise hand movements, which were known as somatic components.

Raven needed an opportunity to escape, and Gwendolyn needed a distraction to make that possible. She steadied herself, tried to block out the panicked cries coming from her daughter, reached into her satchel and began flipping through the stack of minor casting-cards she brought along with her.

Payback is a Witch

She landed on and briefly considered using a thaumaturgy spell to produce a sound loud enough to divert the attackers' attention but quickly dismissed the idea when she glanced up and her eyes landed on an overgrown section of brightly colored Goldenrod plants. Buzzing lazily from one flower to the next, she saw a small swarm of fuzzy black and yellow honeybees and decided that a Compulsion spell would do the trick. She quickly found the compulsion casting-card, glanced over it, and thanked Goddess that only spoken word and somatic components was needed, luckily, no material components were necessary to cast Compulsion.

With a little time and the right components, she could have conjured a whole insect plague, but time was of the essence and immediate action was pivotal if she was to be implemental in saving her daughter. Gwendolyn made a quick mental note and would definitely keep the plague idea in the back of her mind for later use.

Though components were not necessary, Gwendolyn knew she could use the Goldenrod flowers to form a stronger connection between herself and her soon to be minions. She quickly pulled off a thick cluster of the vibrant yellow flowers, which she crushed between the palms of her hands, she then reached out and snagged one of the honeybees midflight as it floated passed her.

Understandably aggravated at being derailed from its vital job of collecting nectar for the collective hive, as well as its equally important but unbeknownst role of pollination of flora within the local ecosystem, the bee buzzed angrily within the confines of Gwendolyn's circled fist. However, it made no attempt to defend itself by stinging her. Gwendolyn brought the fist containing the frenzied captive to her lips and urgently sounded off her spell while performing the somatic gesture necessary to cast compulsion with her free hand.

"Aristaeus, faithful keeper of stinging bee, grant power over swarm to me." When the last word was whispered, the manic insect immediately went still and Gwendolyn knew her spell was cast.

She laid flat the palm of her hand and stared at the tiny bee. The enchanted insect stared back, sunlight glinting off the tiny globes of its compound eyes while awaiting its orders. Gwendolyn parted her lips and the bee took flight, buzzing directly into her mouth and settling upon her tongue. With the three Ocelli eyes atop its head, the bee detected the change in light as Gwendolyn closed her mouth, enshrouding the creature in darkness. Her eyes snapped shut at the same time and the connection was complete. In an instant, Gwendolyn assumed the role of queen of the colony, then with a casual wave of her hand in the direction of the Goldenrod flowers, she halted the workers, which were busy as a bee, collecting pollen and nectar. In unison, the bees—about ten in total—effortlessly rotated in midair to face Raven's attackers, and with no more than a thought, Gwendolyn put her minions to work.

3

The bees departed like ten tiny AH-64 Apache combat helicopters in the direction of the tangle of human flesh as Raven did her best to fight back while the men held her down. All of them fondling and groping at her in a state of heightened sexual frenzy. Ryan savagely ripped Raven's skirt and undergarments off, then wasted no time shoving his face between her legs as Jason and Marcus held them spread open for him, and just as his tongue probed into her sex, he felt a tiny bolt of lightning strike the back of his neck.

Ryan sprang up from between Raven's legs like a jack in the box and slapped the back of his neck. "What the fuck was that?" he exclaimed while examining the black and yellow mess in the middle of his palm. He could still feel the stinger pumping venom into the back of his neck when all hell broke loose.

Payback is a Witch

Out of nowhere, the bees began dive-bombing the men, and in an instant, their sexual frenzy turned into one of panic, with the men flailing their arms around their heads trying to fend off the attacking insects.

Jason, who was holding onto one of Raven's legs, looked around in a panic at the tiny swarm of bees as they buzzed angrily around his head and he shouted, "I'm getting the fuck outta here, I allergic to bees. You guys are on your own." He then released his hold on Raven's leg and bolted off into the woods. Marcus was hot on Jason's heels, swatting at his hair when two angry bees landed upon and were tangled within the trendy afro he was currently sporting.

With skillful precision, a second bee landed on Ryan's bottom eyelid, and without hesitation, jammed its stinger home. Once again, Ryan instinctively swatted at it, smashing the insect against his cheek and accidentally smearing it up towards his eye. This impulsive action was twofold—a blessing and a curse at the same time. A blessing because he managed to pull the bee's stinger out, thus preventing more venom from being pumped into his eyelid, and a curse because Ryan did not close his eyes quickly enough and bits and pieces of the pulverized insect found their way into his socket. He could feel the prickly spindle hairs on the bee's segmented legs scraping across his cornea as easily as he could the torn and broken forewing, which managed to get lodged under his upper eyelid. All of this was enough to cause him to abandon his attack on Raven, and soon, he too disappeared into the woods.

The remaining bees focused their attack on Charles and Brian, dashing in and zipping back out, which finally forced the men to release their grip on Raven's arms in an attempt to protect them from the incoming assault. Raven seized the opportunity, scrambled up from the ground, sprinted off into the bayou, and within seconds, she was lost from sight amongst the knobby trunks of the moss-ridden cypress trees.

The brothers contemplated pursuing Raven but Gwendolyn renewed the fury of her attack, so all thoughts of the pursuit were lost as the men found themselves fleeing from the small swarm in the opposite direction.

"This isn't over, bitch," Charles shouted into the woods. "We're coming for the both of you. You hear me!"

Gwendolyn smiled inwardly as she watched the men being chased by the swarm until they were well out of sight. She opened her mouth, and once again, the bee's Ocelli eyes detected the change in shadows. The insect took flight and exited Gwendolyn's mouth, and with that, the connection to her minions severed and Gwendolyn began to make her way back to the cottage where she was sure Raven would be awaiting her return.

4

It was just after dusk as Gwendolyn lounged lazily in her favorite chair next to an open window, listening to the sounds of the nighttime bayou as it slowly came to life. She watched expressively as Raven paced angrily back and forth across the floor of the cottage.

"How fuckin' dare those low life thugs put their filthy hands on me?" Raven fumed. "Do they have any idea who I am, who *we* are?"

"Calm down, Raven," Gwendolyn soothed. "Things could have been a lot worse."

"Calm down! How can I calm down when I was almost gang raped and those creeps said that they were coming back to finish the job!" Raven said heatedly.

Having seen enough of her daughter

frantically pacing, Gwendolyn stood, took Raven by the hands, and said, "Surely you don't think that we were going to let common street trash get away with putting their hands on you and threatening us, did you?"

Raven visibly relaxed and listened as her mother continued.

"If any of those men come looking for us before we can get to them, they'll learn just how powerful a witch scorned can be," said Gwendolyn. "However, this doesn't mean that we're going to sit idly and wait for them to come knockin'. We're going to hunt them down and pick them off, one after the other, until all of them have paid for their transgression against us."

With this, Gwendolyn retrieved her box of casting-cards and casually flipped through them until she found the Scrying spell. She then instructed Raven to fetch a rather expensive looking silver-plated mirror from their secret Wiccan artifact collection room, which she would use as a speculum to obtain divination. Raven placed the mirror right-side-up on the table, lit a few candles to allow for better lighting, sat opposite her mother, and watched as Gwendolyn began to scry for their victim.

Gwendolyn traced the Wiccan rune for enlightenment in the air, drawing an ever-shrinking spiral above the mirror, symbolizing the journey from lost to found and focused her thoughts on one of the men, she then softly chanted the words for the Scrying spell. *"Mirrors to see, mirrors to show, mirrors reflect my desire to know. Show unto me the one I seek, show unto me, so mote it be."*

The surface of the mirror undulated like the ripple from a stone tossed into the still waters of a pond, and Gwendolyn's reflection was replaced with the face of Ryan. The man's right eye was swollen shut and bruised black and blue from where the bee stung him. He was sitting at one of the local bars, chatting it up with a few of his other friends and drinking. He was obviously well beyond his limit as he was slurring his words.

Able to see the interior décor of the bar Ryan was currently a patron of, Raven whispered to her mother, "I know this bar. I've stopped in a few times during our excursions into town." Gwendolyn gave a disapproving look to her daughter, then turned her focus back to the mirror.

"Give me another one," Ryan said to the cute bartender standing behind the counter.

"I think you've had enough," the woman answered in reply as she snatched Ryan's car keys from where they lay atop the bar. "And you should probably walk home, the night air will do you good. You can come back for these in the morning," she said with a sly smile, dangling Ryan's keys in front of him.

Ryan made a grab for the keys, but in his current inebriated state lacked sufficient motor skills to successfully reclaim them. The bartender easily snatched the keys out of his reach, and then slid them down the front of her shirt. He tried his hardest to argue the point that he was more than sober enough to drive home but she stood firm and he knew that he would be getting no further libation from her, nor would he be getting his keys back.

"Well, fuck you then," Ryan slurred as he knocked over his chair and made his way to use the restroom before walking home to sleep it off.

"Looks like an opportunity has presented itself and we've got to hurry if we're going to cash in on it," Gwendolyn said to Raven as she stood from the table, severing the connection to Ryan. Gwendolyn retrieved a flying ointment, which was a salve, containing a blend of fat and psychotropic herbs. She then adorned a festive neckpiece within which was crafted four great horned owl feathers. Gwendolyn flipped through her casting-cards in an attempt to locate the spells she required, and then exited the cottage with Raven in tow.

When the two reached a relatively clear section of the bayou, which was not laden with overhanging tree boughs, Gwendolyn opened the salve, dipped her fingers into the mixture, and chanted. *"With breath and will, I cast this spell"*. She traced the somatic component, a triangle with an intersecting line denoting its cap upon her daughters' forehead as well as her upon her own and continued. *"With ointment of flight, and feather of night"*, Gwendolyn then pulled a feather from her necklace and slipped it into Raven's hairline. *"Gravity renounce your hold over me".* Stashing the remaining ointment in a satchel she finished, *"light as a feather, so mote it be."*

When Gwendolyn spoke the last word of the flying spell she gave a knowing wink to her daughter and said, "Broomsticks are so cliché." She then lifted her face skyward, at which point her feet left the ground. Gwendolyn rose until she was hovering just above the tree line and waited for Raven to join her. Raven mimicked her mother's somatic gesture, then spoke the words for the flying spell, after which she floated up to join Gwendolyn and added, "Not to mention the splinters we'd get." Both women laughed aloud and with a slight adjustment of their bodies, they began to soar off in the

direction of town, with Raven leading
the way.

5

The humid Louisiana air felt almost tangible and hit Ryan like a ton of bricks when he exited the bar, causing the world to spin. Bile began to rise from the pit of his stomach so he paused, resting against one of the cars in the parking lot to steady himself. After a few seconds, the vertigo cleared enough for him to push off from the car and begin his journey home.

Ryan made his way out of the parking lot, and soon, the garish neon lights of the bar's billboard were left behind and the darkness of night surrounded him. The streetlights were few, and far between as Ryan staggered towards his home, and traffic on the road at this time of night was relatively sparse. He was so preoccupied with trying not to lose his balance and go tumbling into one of the shallow ditches lining the sides of the road, he failed to notice the two shadows quietly trailing him.

"Fuck, I gotta piss again," Ryan said to no one in particular as he stepped off the road, unzipped his pants and released a stream of built-up urine from his bladder. He stood there with his head tilted back looking up at the trees overhead for few seconds until he saw what he thought were headlights quickly approaching. Just then, five dazzling white orbs of light surrounded and started circling him like gigantic fireflies.

"What the fuck!" Ryan exclaimed as he released hold of his penis and started swatting at the flying lights, causing him to catch his foot on a raised tree root and go crashing to the ground, his flaccid penis still spurting a heavy arch of golden urine angled upwards, drenching his clothing and face with lukewarm piss. Ryan landed with a thud hard on his ass, which forced him to involuntarily swallow down some of his own bodily fluids. He clenched his pelvic floor muscles to stop the flow of urine, sat up, and spat out the rest of the salty-tasting liquid as he looked around in confusion. He could see the lights flittering amongst the trees about one hundred feet in front of him. The orbs coalesced into one and assumed a vaguely feminine form, which began to move deeper into the woods.

"What the hell?" Ryan whispered to himself as he stood and zipped his pants. He wiped the back of his sleeve across his face in a feeble attempt to dry the piss that was still dripping from his brow and stared at the glowing woman in the distance, who seemed to be motioning for him to follow her.

"I must be drunker than I thought," Ryan said as he began vigorously rubbing his eyes, convinced that he must be hallucinating. The luminescent woman sauntered seductively deeper into the woods and Ryan followed, thinking to himself that the glow must be a trick of the moonlight shining through the thick canopy of the treetops overhead, and knowing that when he did catch up with whoever this teasing bitch was, one way or another, he was getting laid.

***

After casting the Dancing Lights spell and quickly memorizing another, both Gwendolyn and Raven followed Ryan from a safe distance, baiting the intoxicated man onward and deeper into the marshland. When certain they had led their victim to a secluded enough area where they would not be interrupted, Gwendolyn halted the luminous decoy and allowed Ryan to catch up with it.

Ryan made it to within twenty feet of the figure when, without warning, the glowing woman exploded and disassembled back into five individual white orbs which floated lazily through the air, shedding dim light within a ten-foot radius from where they hovered. Gwendolyn and Raven stepped out of the shadows and into the glow.

Ryan's eyes widened with recognition as he backed up a step. "What the fuck is going on?" Ryan spat at the two women, then reversed his action and took a menacing step towards them, all thoughts of the glowing woman completely forgotten.

"Oh, I get it, obviously this bitch wants me to finish the job I started earlier, and I guess mom wants some of this dick too." Ryan continued, grabbing a hand full of his crotch.

He took another step forward as Gwendolyn drew an intricate arcane symbol in the air then thrust her hand towards Ryan. She sounded the words for the Ray of Sickness spell, from memory, and a sickly greenish beam of energy burst forth from her palm and hit Ryan squarely in the chest.

Ryan yelped, stumbled backwards, and glanced down at his chest but it was unchanged and all was as before. He regained his composure and continued to advance towards the duo. "And just what the fuck was that supposed to be?" Ryan asked mockingly, "some kind of spooky ass spell or some shit?"

"As a matter of fact, yes, that's exactly what it was," replied Gwendolyn with a malicious look on her face. "Seeing as how you like to drink so much, I thought a touch of alcohol poisoning would make for quite an amusing punishment for what you and your friends did to my beautiful daughter."

Ryan let loose a roar of laughter and said, "you fucking bitches are crazy. What we did earlier to your whore of a daughter ain't shit compared to what I'm about to do to the both of you."

Ryan took two steps forward, and suddenly, his world once again turned upside down. The drunkenness he felt earlier seemed to rush back into him, only this time, it felt multiplied tenfold, as if he had been binge drinking and taking shot after shot of tequila for hours on end. His skin paled, taking on an almost bluish tint as his body temperature plummeted. He grabbed his head, stumbled, and fell to the ground in a heap. The abrupt and severe re-inebriation caused instant Gastritis as the lining of his stomach became irritated, inflamed, and began to erode.

Nausea—the likes of which he had never known before—hit him and made the world spin once more, then he screamed and crunched into the fetal position as white-hot daggers of abdominal pain assaulted him, causing him to projectile vomit, and covering his chest and clothes in a gut soup of mushed-up, half-digested chicken wings, spit, and stomach juice.

"What's happenin' to me?" Ryan slurred when he was finally able to take in a breath. His head lulled back and forth and his eyes rolled up and into their sockets as he rolled around in the soil like a newborn infant. He tried to stand but barely made it to his knees before drunkenly tumbling back to the ground.

He was just on the verge of passing out when Gwendolyn waved her hands in the air, ending her spell and quelling the tempest raging within Ryan's body. The nausea and agony he was feeling slowly began to subside.

"Please, no more," Ryan sobbed as he wallowed on the ground, covered in vomit and dirt. "I'm sorry. I'm so sorry."

Until now, Raven stood by passively enjoying the show, and allowing her mother to avenge her, but Ryan's pathetic begging was just the fuel she needed to prompt her into action. She repeated the steps her mother did, extending her hand towards Ryan and sounding out the words for the Ray of Sickness spell. Ryan let out a blood curdling "NOOOO," just as another sickly green beam of light made contact with him.

"Let's see how he does with food poisoning," Raven said with a wicked grin splitting her face in two.

Ryan began sobbing uncontrollably and managed to climb to his hands and knees, then stopped in his tracks as he began to hear and feel a low baritone grumbling building deep within his guts. "No, please," he moaned pitifully as the stomach cramping intensified. The pain in his stomach was so severe when it reached its crescendo that it once again forced him to involuntarily spew forth bloody, gastric fluids and the remaining partly-digested food that was left in his stomach. The vile mixture splattered wetly into the dirt in front of him as he clutched his stomach, then another wave of intense cramping hit him, causing him to lose balance and collapse face-first into his own regurgitation.

The impact of his face smacking into the wet ground along with the abdomen cramping loosened his bowels and he flooded his jeans with blood-streaked diarrhea. The watery, foul-smelling stools exploded from his rectum in a torrent, quickly turning the seat of his pants a muddy brown color and running down the back of his legs like a kid plummeting down a waterslide. Ryan fell to his side and lay there, bathed in his own filth, still clinching at his stomach, which felt as if it was being pinched and squeezed in a vice-like grip, crying pitifully as his body temperature now began to rise.

The shock to Ryan's body from fast-tracked alcohol poisoning to severe food poisoning was too much for him to handle and caused abrupt and abnormal electrical and chemical changes in his brain. His body began to convulse violently as the seizure took hold of him. Almost immediately, Ryan lost consciousness as one last convulsion of his body caused him to flip and land face-down into the puddle of his vomit where he lay unmoving until he asphyxiated in his own spew.

Gwendolyn and Raven impassively watched Ryan's punishment unfold and when they were sure he had expired, Raven stepped up to Ryan's corpse and whispered through clinched teeth. "I hope you rot in hell."

Gwendolyn placed a gentle hand on her daughters' shoulder and said, "Let's go home now. We still have a lot of work to do."

With a wave of her hand, she dismissed the glowing orbs, which slowly faded away and winked out of existence, leaving the two women enshrouded in darkness. Gwendolyn and Raven repeated the steps for the Flying spell and once again, both women rose into the air and zipped off in the direction of their cottage.

6

The next night found the witches back at the scrying mirror. They watched Marcus on and off as he went about his day. They watched as the handsome African American boy woke early, showered, then dressed and went off to class, then they caught up with him again later in the day as he worked feverishly in the kitchen as a cook at one of the local restaurants. By the time 10 pm rolled around, Marcus was back at home relaxing in front of the television, watching the 1973 version of *Don't Be Afraid of the Dark*, one of his favorite horror flicks, with his on-again, off-again girlfriend, Alicia, who was a server at the same restaurant as Marcus.

Marcus's parents were away on vacation and he lived above the garage in the guesthouse behind his parents' home, so he pretty much had free rein of the property. He and Alicia made their way back to his pad after they got off from work and he was feeling horny as fuck, having knocked back a few drinks after clocking out. Alicia being clad in nothing more than panties and one of Marcus's baggy t-shirts did nothing to help the tightening in his crotch as his dick hardened.

"Why don't we just put this movie on hold?" said Marcus as he picked up the remote control and pressed pause. He then climbed on top of Alicia and started kissing her on the neck.

"And just what do you think you're doing?" asked Alicia teasingly. "You said we were coming here to watch a movie," she continued.

"Well, I'd much rather watch you suck this dick," Marcus said with a devilish grin on his face. "But, if you'd rather finish the movie, that's fine with me," he said deviously as he began to climb off.

Alicia grabbed Marcus and pulled him back on top of her. "Get back here," she said as the two began to kiss. Alicia parted her mouth and Marcus slipped his tongue in and kissed her deeply. After a few minutes of passionate kissing, Alicia laid a hand atop Marcus's shoulders and pushed him down, which was her way of telling him that before he would be getting any head, he would be giving some. This was all the incentive Marcus needed as he honestly enjoyed orally pleasuring Alicia. The taste of her was intoxicating and he was obviously very good at it because whenever he went down on her, she would orgasm, without fail.

Marcus nibbled his way down Alicia's neck, lingering for a while when he reached her breast. He focused on her tits, aggressively squeezing, pinching, biting, and sucking on both of them. From the first time they had sex, which was actually on the first night they met, Marcus made it clear to Alicia that he was exceedingly dominant and that sex between them would be aggressive and more often wild than mild. After a few minutes of listening to Alicia's erotic whimpering as he pleasured her chest, he continued his journey downward. When he reached her bush, he wasted no time in sliding her panties down as he began to please her with his very talented tongue.

Marcus's tongue trailed down, briefly passing over Alicia's clitoral hood and then stopped when he reached the tiny gland of flesh right below the hood. He spent a good deal of time and effort stroking, sucking, and licking the marble of flesh, which was bursting with sensitive nerve endings. Marcus focused his attention on Alicia's clitoris, building her up with anticipation to what he knew was sure to be multiple and very powerful orgasms. Eventually, he abandoned his exploration of her clit as his tongue continued its downward journey, passing briefly over her urethral opening and finally coming to a halt when he reached her vagina.

Alicia could feel the warmth of Marcus's breath on her sex, which only heightened her eagerness to have him inside of her. Without warning, he slid his snake-like tongue deep inside her, licking up and down with consistent, rhythmic movements. When his spit and her juices had her sufficiently lubed, he took one of his fingers, placed it between her labia, then slowly inserted it and began finger fucking her while eating her out at the same time, which brought about Alicia's first climax of the night.

He had skillfully unclothed himself while he was pleasuring Alicia with his tongue, so he was ready for her when she lustfully moaned to him,

"I want you inside of me."

With one fluid motion, he abandoned his oral exploration of her genitals, climbed up her body until their hips were adjacent, and roughly rammed his swollen member deep inside her, the savageness of his entry bringing about Alicia's second orgasm of the night.

The two fucked ferociously and in multiple positions until Marcus was unable to hold back any longer. He announced that he was about to cum and he did so, releasing deep inside of her, which culminated in Alicia's third and final orgasm. When the session was over, both were exhausted and sweating profusely.

After a few minutes, Marcus turned to Alicia and said, "I've got to get some sleep and I know you have to get up early for work in the morning," which was his way of slyly dismissing her for the night.

This was just fine with Alicia as she was more than satisfied and understood that their relationship these days was more sexual in nature than it was girlfriend and boyfriend. "Yeah, I guess you're right," she replied as she got out of bed and proceeded to get dressed. "I guess I'll see you in a few days when you're back on the schedule at work," Alicia continued.

"Sounds good," Marcus replied.

The two said their goodbyes as Marcus walked her downstairs, then watched as she strolled down the driveway, got into her car, and drove away. Marcus glanced at the wetness still covering his dick as he walked back upstairs and said aloud to himself, "I hope that bitch didn't give me an STD," then laughed out loud. It was a little after midnight when he resumed his movie and watched it until it lulled him off to sleep.

Gwendolyn and Raven smiled at one another as yet another opportunity presented itself. "I've got this one," Raven said as she stood from the table upon which the scrying mirror rested. She walked over and began flipping through their collection of casting-cards, looking for the spells she needed. After locating the desired cards and donning accessories containing the required components, the women once again exited the cottage into the muggy nighttime air of the Louisiana bayou.

Raven reached into a pouch hanging from her side and withdrew two small shavings of licorice root, one of which she passed to her mother and the other she kept for herself. Both women placed the shavings into their mouths and tucked them into the side of their jaws like chewing tobacco, then recited the words for a spell called Haste. A pale, ghostly light outlined the feet of both women and they immediately set out in the direction of town, moving at double their normal speed.

The witches' cottage was about six miles from the edge of town, and whereas the journey would normally take the pair about two hours to complete, they arrived at their destination in just under an hour. Raven's knowledge of the city, combined with the spying they did earlier in the day, helped the witches navigate to Marcus's place of residence with relative ease. They emerged from the darkness of the tree line surrounding the property and glared up at the window to what they assumed to be Marcus's bedroom.

"Ok, daughter, and just how do you expect to gain entry to the home?" Gwendolyn asked Raven.

Raven smiled and said, "I'm going

to knock, of course, how else would you expect us to get in?" With that, she pulled out one of the casting-cards from her satchel, glanced over it, and quietly knocked on the door three times as she spoke the words for a spell simply called Knock. There was a barely audible click as the door's lock disengaged. Raven took hold of the handle, gave it a gentle twist, and the door silently swung open.

"Well done," said Gwendolyn approvingly as they moved in silence up the stairs. When they reached the landing, the stairwell opened to a small living room adorned with rather basic furniture, typical of what you would fine in bachelors' pad. Straight ahead was a small kitchen, and to the left through another door a bedroom and tiny bathroom

With a gesture, Raven halted her mother in the living room; she then waved the palm of her hand across her face and quietly spoke the words for the Disguise-Self spell. *"Now a canvas I wipe clean, only what I visualize shall be seen."* With the final word, her image shimmered then altered into a splitting image of Alicia.

Gwendolyn beamed with pride at the cunningness of her daughter. "Now what?"

"Now, you hide yourself from view and enjoy the show," Raven replied in Alicia's voice.

Gwendolyn fiddled with a trendy bracelet wrapped around her wrist from which dangled a small charm of a single eyelash encased in gum Arabic—one component she kept with her at all times. She rubbed the charm with her free hand, while chanting the words for the Invisibility spell and instantly began to disappear from sight. One minute she was there, and the next, she wasn't. The only evidence of Gwendolyn being present was an empty beer can as it floated up from the living room table, then glided spookily, disappearing around the corner and into the bedroom.

Raven, in the guise of Alicia, readied herself and casually walked into the bedroom. Marcus was still naked and lying in the bed, sound asleep. Alicia walked over, sat on the edge of the bed, and gently shook Marcus awake.

"Marcus, Marcus, wake up, I need to talk to you," she softly said.

Marcus groggily opened his eyes, and startled, he let out a little yelp of fright when he saw Alicia sitting on the side of his bed.

"What the hell are you doing here? You scared the fuck outta me," he said as they both began to laugh.

"You left the door unlocked,"

Alicia replied. "I knocked but you didn't hear me so I let myself in."

"Oh, ok," Marcus sighed, wiping sleep from his eyes. He reached out, took Alicia by the hand, and pulled her down onto the bed. "Well, since you're here…" Marcus said, a lustful smile tugging at the edge of his lips.

Alicia allowed herself to be pulled into the bed and let Marcus cradle her in his arms as the spell she selected as his judgment required her to make physical contact with her target. She wrapped her arms around his neck, signing the somatic component behind his back as she unintelligibly muttered into his ear the words for the Contagion spell.

"What'd you say?" Marcus asked. "I couldn't hear you."

"Oh, never mind, it was nothing," Alicia replied dismissively.

Payback is a Witch

Marcus began planting kisses on her neck and lips. She gently rebuked his advances and hesitantly said, "I have to talk to you about something." Marcus absentmindedly began scratching at his crotch as he waited for Alicia to continue.

She looked away shamefully and continued, "I don't really know how to tell you this, but when I got home after leaving here I checked my voicemail. There was a call from my doctor," she paused, twisting nervously at the bedsheets, tears glistening wetly in the corners of her eyes, thinking to herself that she should win an academy award for her acting aptitude. She continued, with a tremble in her voice. "Last week, I wasn't feeling great so I went in for a checkup. The doctor said he was going to run some tests and get back to me. The results came back and he left word saying that I have a very aggressive and anti-biotic resistant strain of Syphilis."

Marcus's eyes went wide and he looked down at his penis, which immediately began to lose its rigidity when he heard the news. Marcus felt a slight tingling in his groin and right before his eyes, almost as if by magic, small, painless chancres begin to rise on the head and shaft of his now flaccid member, as well as around the corners of his mouth. The tops of the ulcerations covering his infected penis swelled until they split and began to ooze as the magic of Alicia's Contagion spell progressed the symptoms of the primary syphilis she infected him with exponentially.

Marcus sprang up from the bed and ran into the bathroom. "What the fuck have you given me?" he shouted, examining the rising bumps in a panic.

Alicia ran behind him and stood in

the doorway of the bathroom, alligator tears running down her cheeks. "I'm sorry," she replied, seemingly in as much of a panic as Marcus was.

Marcus watched in horror as the disease progressed to its secondary stage. Scaly, reddish-brown rashes manifested over his entire body, he swooned and grabbed onto the bathroom sink to prevent himself from falling over when a wave of fatigue washed over him. His throat was sore and a vague feeling of general discomfort began to spread throughout his entire body. A tingling sensation in the back of his throat prompted him to open his mouth and look into the mirror above the sink. He gagged when he saw numerous pus-filled sores covering the roof of his mouth. One of the abscesses ruptured before his eyes, dripping sickly yellowish pus from the top of his mouth onto his tongue. Marcus salivated as vomit rose in the back of his throat. He reflexively swallowed it back down with the chaser of pus, which had gathered within the depression running lengthwise down center of his tongue. He retched again.

Marcus glared at Alicia as she stood in the doorway; a malicious grin cocked her mouth askew. "Don't just stand there smiling, fuckin' do something, call somebody!" Marcus said through clenched teeth. "This is your fault, you nasty fuckin' bitch!" he scolded.

"Hmmm... I'm confused, was I a nasty bitch when you and your roguish friends tried to gang rape me in the bayou just a few days ago?" Alicia asked sneeringly.

"What the fuck are you talking about?" Marcus asked with a confused look on his face.

Alicia dismissed her glamour with

a wave of her hands. Her visage shimmered as the façade faded and was replaced by her true form. Standing behind her daughter, Gwendolyn sharpened into view as she dismissed her Invisibility spell.

Marcus paled even further and his eyes went wide with panic at seeing both women magically appear before him. He tried to call out for help but the magically accelerated STD aggressively invaded his nervous system and disrupted the impulses to his voice box, and nothing more than a hoarse croak escaped his pale lips.

The most destructive stage of the disease set upon him with ferocity as large spongy, tumor-like growths began to break out over his body and genitals. The necrotic center of each mass was moist, raw, and tender to the touch. One particularly nasty growth spouted on his scrotum and erupted, secreting blood-tinted puss that ran down his inner thigh and pooled around his feet.

Marcus mustered the last bit of remaining strength he had and tried to make a break for the door, hoping to push his way past Raven and her mother and sprint out of the house, but numbness spread through his entire body as the neurosyphilis began to affect his spinal cord, causing a complete loss of muscle coordination. He lost all feeling in his legs and slipped in the puss, which had accumulated on the floor around his feet. There was a sickening crack as he smashed face-first into the porcelain sink, breaking his jaw and knocking out a few perfectly pearlescent teeth in the process before crashing to the floor in an infected heap. He was in agonizing pain and bleeding profusely from his mouth as well as the numerous ulcerations covering his body.

"Who's the nasty bitch now?" Raven

said, crinkling her brow in disgust. She glanced over her shoulder to her mother and coldly said, "He'll be dead by morning. I think we're done here." Gwendolyn nodded in acknowledgment, then both mother and daughter backed away from the growing pool of blood and puss on the bathroom floor and exited the house, locking the door behind them on the way out. As a precaution, Raven removed the beer can her mother picked up upon entering the apartment and wiped the doorknob free of any possible fingerprints.

When both women were safely within the blackness of the woods surrounding the home and prior to recasting the Haste spell, Raven huffed and said to her mother, "we've got to have a more expeditious way of traveling."

"Agreed," Gwendolyn replied. "A Teleport spell should do the trick. We'll have to do a little recon work and obtain a few necessary objects of association prior to being able to use teleport, but I think it'll be worth the legwork." With this, both women recast Haste and sped off towards home.

7

"I'm telling you those bitches had something to do with this," Charles said to Jason and Brian.

It was just a little over a week since the police found Marcus's nearly unrecognizable body lying bloated and swarming with maggots on his bathroom floor after receiving a call from Alicia informing them that he hadn't shown up for work. It was Saturday afternoon and the trio of friends were hanging out at the apartment Charles rented with his brother, Brian, kicking back playing video games.

"How is that even possible?" Jason replied. "The police report said that there was no evidence of forced entry and that Marcus was found in his bathroom dead as a result of an accident. So, what makes you think they could possibly have anything to do with his death?"

"It's just a feeling I have," Charles answered. "Don't you think it's strange that first, Marcus is found dead in his apartment, and now no one has heard from or seen Ryan in over a week and a half? I'm telling you something's not right."

"Ryan's probably hermitted away in a hotel room on a binger drowning his sorrows," Jason responded. "I'm sure he'll sober up and make an appearance in the next couple of days."

"Maybe," Charles said doubtfully, "but I'm still going to do some investigating of my own to see if I can figure out what the fuck is going on.

"Good luck with that," said Jason in a snarky tone as he picked himself up off the couch and made his way towards the door, thinking to himself that Charles was wasting his time in pursuit of something that was sure to prove futile. "I'm gonna bounce, I'll catch up with you losers later."

Jason exited the apartment, jumped into his 2014 Dodge Charger, and sped off towards home. Being the most successful of the group, Jason was able to land an entry-level position at a reputable law firm located in New Orleans, and with the money he managed to save as well as a small donation from his well-off parents, fifteen minutes later, he was pulling into the driveway of the modest, middle-class one-story home he recently purchased. He stepped out of the car, went inside, plopped down on the couch, and began flipping through channels on the boob tube. After idly channel surfing for a solid twenty minutes, he abandoned all hope of finding anything worth watching and picked up his cell phone. He spent another twenty minutes scrolling through TikTok, which he also quickly lost interest in as nothing new or noteworthy was trending.

"Fuck this," Jason said to no one in particular, pushed himself up from the couch, and headed towards the back yard. He was horribly bored and the prospects for finding anything to entertain himself with was looking grim. He opened the sliding glass doors and was immediately assaulted by the oppressiveness of the summertime heat. Being born and raised in Louisiana, he had by now grown quite accustomed to the yearly heatwaves but today was a real scorcher.

"This heat is fucking miserable," Jason said, wiping the sweat that was already beginning to accumulate on his forehead. His eyes roamed over the immaculately manicured backyard, with its impeccably maintained landscaping, and finally converged on the sparkling pool at its center—all of which was surrounded by an eight-foot-tall Cedar wood privacy fence. The back fence opposite the sliding glass door on the other side of the pool was overgrown with Night Jasmine in addition to numerous other pollinating perennials. Jason inhaled deeply, breathing in the intoxicating scent of the Jasmine, which filled the air, and once again contemplated having his gardener dispatch the foliage adorning the fence due to the possibility of a life-threatening allergic reaction from one of the many honeybees that frequented his yard in search of pollen and nectar.

Sweat stung his eyes as it dripped from his brow—Jason blinked the sweat away and decided that a refreshing dip in the pool was the perfect cure for his boredom as well as the most effective way to escape the unrelenting heatwave. Jason stripped down to his boxers, grabbed his phone, Bose Bluetooth speaker, and Epipen, just in case, and headed outside.

8

Over the past few days, Gwendolyn kept a vigilant watch on Jason's home, as well the apartment shared by Charles and Brian via the scrying mirror, while Raven busied herself locating and traveling to Jason's place of residence, under the cloak of darkness, to collect the necessary item she would use for association and to familiarize herself with the surroundings in order to be able to successfully use the Teleportation spell. When Gwendolyn spied Jason floating lazily in the seclusion of his yard, she knew that yet another opportunity was at hand.

"Raven, ready yourself, I think it's time for a little payback," Gwendolyn called out to her daughter as she rose from the table and began flipping through her catalogue of casting-cards. Upon locating the desired cards, Gwendolyn quickly scanned over them while slipping on a few component bracelets—she then stashed the card along with one prefabricated component i a multi-compartment utility belt she wor around her waist. By the time she foun all she needed, Raven had alread retrieved the watch she collected fro Jason's home. She stepped up to he mother and asked, "Are we ready?" a which point Gwendolyn gave an affirmative nod but not before passing one ver important casting-card to her daughter "Read this and accessorize accordingly, she instructed Raven.

Raven quickly packed on the necessary incidentals, strapped the watch around her wrist, and gingerly took her mother by the hand. She closed her eyes and began to visualize the layout of Jason's home then chanted. *"In this time and in the hour, I call upon an ancient power. Move us two through time, through space. Move from here to there, post haste."*

When the last word was uttered,

there was a sound like a thunderclap as air rushed in to fill the space previously occupied by the women when they vanished. In Jason's bedroom, paper and other small items toppled over as the room was assaulted by a push of displaced wind accompanying the witches' reappearance.

"Nice landing," Gwendolyn praised as she took a few seconds to orient herself to her new surroundings. She walked over to the window and peeked through the blinds to see Jason swimming lazily back and forth across the pool. Gwendolyn retrieved the casting-cards from her belt and quickly memorized the spells she selected for this occasion, then motioned for Raven to do the same. When the spells were committed to memory, both women made their way to the backyard to find that Jason had abandoned the refreshing water and was now lounging on a large pool float in the middle of the pool.

Payback is a Witch

Gwendolyn and Raven noisily steppe
onto the patio, causing Jason to snap ou
of the peaceful cocoon of serenity he wa
encompassed within. He instantly spran
into a sitting position atop th
floatation device when he saw the wome
emerge from his living room an
exclaimed, "what the hell! What the fuc
are you doing here and how the hell di
you bitches get into my house?" He
started paddling the pool float towards
the end of the pool and continued. "
suggest you don't hang around and get the
fuck off of my property before I get out
of this pool. I swear, if I get my hands
on you, I'm gonna beat the shit out of
both of you bitches," he threatened in a
low throaty growl.

Gwendolyn smiled mockingly and
pointed her left hand, which was adorned
with a bracelet made from a small loop of
leather, towards Jason, simultaneously
drawing the Wiccan symbol for air with
her right hand as she chanted her
invocation. *"Goddess of flight, mistress*

of air, leave him floating in despair. Rise him up, for all to see. Lift him up, so mote it be."

When she spoke the last word of the spell, she slowly lifted her left hand. As her hand rose, so too did Jason. With a look of confusion on his face, Jason lifted up from the pool float and hovered two feet above the sparkling water, held aloft by Gwendolyn's Levitation spell.

Jason flailed about in the air, the look of confusion on his face turning to one of fear and panic. "How the fuck are you doing this?" he shouted. "Put me the fuck down, right now! Help! Somebody please help me!" he yelled.

"Quiet him," Gwendolyn prompted her daughter. Understanding the urgency of the situation, Raven immediately sprang into action and quickly sounded off the words for a spell of silence. When the last word was spoken, Raven snapped her hand to her face to cover her

mouth, and in an instant, Jason's crie
for help went unvoiced. Though his mout
moved and he went red-faced with th
effort, no sound exited the 20-foo
sphere of silence he was now encase
within.

"Speak up, boy," Gwendoly
mocked as Jason continued his ineffectiv
struggling and unheard protest. She kne
that her repartee with Jason fell on dea
ears due to the fact that the Silenc
spell was reciprocal. Just as she an
Raven were silenced to Jason's frantic
shouting, she knew that he too wa
deafened to anything she might have t
say to him. With this in mind, Gwendolyn
reached into one of the compartments on
her waist pouch and withdrew a plastic
bag containing a smear of animal fat, a
few granules of sugar, and a handful of
kernels of grain. Gwendolyn traced a
cryptic ideogram in the air, held the bag
aloft and spoke the words for a spell she
was keeping in reserve for just the right
occasion. When the final word was

articulated, Gwendolyn threw the package to the ground whereupon it erupted, spilling forth an insect plague comprised of hundreds of Africanized Honey Bees. The frenzied storm of yellow and black bees filled the air, buzzing aggressively back and forth, but never alighting upon Raven or Gwendolyn and never leaving the boundaries of Jason's backyard.

Jason's eyes went wide with fright when he saw the multitude of bees buzzing all around him and resumed his pointless struggle to free himself with vigor.

"Do it, mother, make this mother-fucker sorry for ever laying his filthy hands on me," Raven said through clenched teeth.

Gwendolyn shot a reproachful look in her daughters' direction at the use of such foul language but was all too happy to oblige and shifted her focus to the manic swarm of insects that were scattered throughout the yard, doing what

bees do best. On cue, each member of th
swarm ceased their individual agendas an
began to gather in a nightmarish insec
conga line, flying counter-clockwis
around the yard. The circling swar
drawing ever tighter, eventuall
surrounding Jason, who was still hel
aloft by Gwendolyn's spell in a buzzin
cyclone of yellow and black. Jaso
struggled in vain, arms and leg
thrashing about comically, mouth openin
and closing in silent screams, when,
without warning, the swarm attacked.

The swarm collectively slammed int
Jason with such force that it pushed hin
backwards through the air. His body
convulsed violently when a multitude of
barbed stingers penetrated his sun-tanned
skin. The water-soluble venom spread
quickly through his body as the proteins
within said venom, along with his severe
allergy to the venom, triggered an almost
immediate response of his immune system,
resulting in intense burning pain and
swelling. To his dismay, Jason's mouth

opened in pointless screams of agony, at which point a handful of bees filed in and began jamming their stingers into his soft fleshy tongue which rapidly began to bloat like a salted slug, compelling a few of the frantic insects to crawl to the back of his throat and inch their way down his esophagus.

As quickly as the attack started, it was over and the bees fled from Jason's hovering form in every direction when Gwendolyn dismissed her conjured horde with a flamboyant flourish, ripping their fragile abdomen and leaving behind still pulsating venom sacs as they did. Jason dangled miserably in the air, rising panic visible in his struggles as he clawed chaotically at his neck when his throat and tongue instantly began to swell, further constricting his airway. Nausea rolled through the pit of Jason's belly, causing the congealed contents of his stomach to rocket partway up his esophagus, only to plummet back down upon finding no clear exit from his body.

Bloody bile, a few chunky pieces o
undigested food, along with one of th
bee that scuttled down his gullet manage
to painfully squeeze up through hi
inflamed esophagus, spew out from betwee.
his bloated lips, and splash wetly int
the pool below.

Unable to refuel his body with life-
sustaining oxygen, Jason convulsed in the
grip of silent panic. With his head
throbbing and his lungs feeling as if
they were set ablaze, he began to fall
further and further into a darkness that
threatened to swallow him whole. The
little oxygen trapped in his lungs
moments earlier was spent and Jason's
brain began to fuzz with the onset of
asphyxia. His erratic struggling began
to subside, then, ever so slowly, his
life faded away with a sense of anguish,
more so than pain, leading him into the
darkness.

When all was still, Raven casually
took a seat on the edge of the pool,

dipped her feet into the cooling waters, pouted, and whined. "The ability to conjure an insect swarm still eludes me," Raven said to her mother dejectedly. "Hard as I try, I'm never able to call forth more than a hand full of insects at any given time."

"Patience breeds perfection child," Gwendolyn replied tenderly. "If you recall, there was a time when you could conjure no more than a sneeze with ray of sickness and now look at you. The ease with which you were able to taint Ryan with full-blown food poisoning is nothing short of impressive. You should be proud of yourself daughter, because I'm extremely proud of you." Gwendolyn smiled lovingly at her daughter.

Raven blushed and smiled back modestly, then quickly withdrew her dainty feet from the pool water when she saw excrement seep from beneath Jason's still dripping swimming trunks, slowly trailing its way down his legs and into the water below. Jason's venom-ravaged body hung limply like a child's forgotten marionette, face and body almost unrecognizable due to the amount of bloating and swelling inflicted by the multitude of bee stings. Looking less like Jason and more like a sick and twisted parody of John Merrick, The Elephant Man.

"It appears that vengeance is ours, daughter," said Gwendolyn with a look of satisfaction etched upon her face. "There is still work to be done, we should hurry home." Then, with a nonchalant downward flip of her left hand, Gwendolyn dismissed her Levitation spell and sent Jason's bloodied and bloated body splashing into the shit-stained pool below.

Raven joined her mother at the edge of the pool and took her by the hand. Both women stood silently and watched Jason's lifeless body floating lazily atop the still waters which had begun to tint a muddy shade of maroon from the combination of blood and feces.

"Take us home, daughter," said Gwendolyn.

Raven closed her eyes, visualized the cozy cottage she called home, and chanted the words for the Teleportation spell. Once again, a thunderclap reverberated through the air as both women disappeared in the blink of an eye.

9

Gwendolyn and Raven spent the days following Jason's death basking in the cleverness of their retaliation, periodically spying on Charles and Brian via the scrying mirror and planning their next move. The morning was uncommonly breezy and surprisingly temperate, so Gwendolyn suggested the two spend the day exploring. "We'll make plans for dealing with the final two tonight when we return," Gwendolyn said to her daughter. They packed a light lunch and left the house shortly after finishing breakfast. They ventured deep into the bayou to collect useful components and perfect a couple of new spells, which they believed would be useful when dealing with the brothers. The hours seemed to fly as both mother and daughter lost themselves in the serenity of their surroundings. Sometimes separating from one another in pursuit of personal agendas and other times spending hours together, with Raven listening intently and hanging on to her mother's every word as Gwendolyn communicated vital Wiccan information to her inquisitive offspring.

It was just after sunset and the women were making their way home, escorted by a cacophony of trilling bayou sounds. "Today was a good day," Raven said to her mother with a smile on her face upon entering the house.

Gwendolyn set about illuminating the rooms as well as unburdening herself from the multitude of accessories she donned prior to leaving for the day's excursion, and replied with a smile of her own. "I agree."

She removed her satchel, which was practically overflowing with the resources she collected throughout the day, in addition to disrobing herself

from the multiple bracelets she wore an
a fashionable-looking couture neckpiec
she recently fabricated, she then walke
into the kitchen and called out to he
daughter, "Are you hungry? I know I am."

Raven responded with an emphatic
"yes, I'm starved."

"Perfect, I'll warm up some gumbo
and make some tea if you'll run out to
the garden to gather a bit of fresh
lavender and mint."

Raven practically squealed with
delight at her mother's offer, as
lavender-mint tea was her all-time
favorite.

"You're the best," Raven said over
her shoulder as she bounded out of the
front door and started to make her way
towards the garden, which was situated in
a clearing about fifty feet from the back
of the house.

Gwendolyn set about retrieving the
Gumbo from the refrigerator and

transferring a small amount of the hearty soup from the large pot it was originally cooked in into a smaller pot which she then placed atop the burner on the stove, she then removed a teapot from the cupboard, filled it with water and set it on the counter. Knowing that it would be a while before Raven's return as the girl could never resist exploring the nighttime bayou, Gwendolyn then decided to check on the brothers one final time. She retrieved the silver-plated mirror from the collection room, placed it right-side-up on the table, traced the Wiccan rune for enlightenment in the air above the mirror, and chanted the words for the Scrying spells. When the last word of the spell was spoken, the surface of the mirror rippled and her reflection was replaced with blackness. Gwendolyn's brow crinkled in confusion as she stared blankly at the mirror and tried to work out what went wrong with her casting.

__10__

The same day, shortly before 2:00

pm, Charles and Brian received a visit from the police delivering a double dose of shockingly bad news. Firstly, telling them that their lifelong friend, Jason, was found dead in his pool as a result of a freak accident, and secondly, informing them that the body of their missing friend, Ryan, was discovered deep in the woods by a couple of kids who were out and about exploring. The detectives spent the next two hours questioning the brothers as they had suspicions of foul play, considering the fact that three of the five men who were often seen running together died within weeks of one another.

Neither Charles nor his brother had any beneficial information to give to the detectives on the death of their friends as neither were sure what was happening or how it was happening. They were convinced that the woman they accosted in the woods weeks earlier and her mother had something to do with what was going on, but it wasn't as if they could voice

these suspicions to the cops without als
informing them of the attempted gang rap
of Raven, so the men sat in relativ
silence, answering any question
presented to them as best as they coul
all while trying not to say too much i
fear of divulging vital information an
accidentally condemning themselves in th
process. Once the detectives wer
convinced that they could gather n
further information from Charles o
Brian, they dismissed themselves, leaving
a card and instructing the men to cal]
should they think of any information that
would be useful to their investigation.

"Now do you believe those bitches
had something to do with all of this?"
Charles asked his brother once they were
alone.

"But how?" queried Brian. "How
could two little ass women get the jump
on and overpower three grown-ass men? It
just doesn't make sense. Unless…" Brian
paused, a wrinkle creasing his forehead.

"Unless what?" Charles prompted his brother to finish his thought process.

"Unless they really are witches," Brian whispered.

Charles let loose a roar of laughter at the implication and regarded his brother quizzically. "Man, get the fuck outta here, you're talking crazy."

"If they're not witches, why don't you tell me what the hell is going on?" Brian countered.

"I don't know, but I do know that there are no such things as witches and magic does not exist. I also know that I'm not about to sit around and let those bitches catch me off guard." Charles said angrily as he exited the room. He returned a few minutes later with a 9mm handgun tucked into the waistband of his pants. "Grab your shit, we're gonna pay those bitches a visit, finish what we started with the daughter, then make both of them sorry they ever fucked with us."

Payback is a Witch

Brian didn't look the least bi happy with his brother's plan but made n objection. He proceeded to gather a fe items he thought might come in handy, an ten minutes later, he and his brothe were making their way towards the bayou As with most of the locals in town who at one time or another, found the courag to make the journey deep into the wood to spy upon the home of the suppose "witch of the woods", both Charles an Brian knew the location of the dwelling and knew that they could locate it with ease. There was no paved road leading to the home and though the men knew the general direction, the journey throug the bayou took them longer than expected and they arrived at their destination just before dusk. They could barely discern the silhouette of the home through the trees in the fading sunlight when Charles halted his brother.

"Let's stop here and wait until dark," he said. "We'll let them settle in for the night, creep up to the house and sneak in through one of the windows. Once inside, you grab the old bitch and tie her up, and I'll take care of the daughter. Once we got them roped and gagged, we'll have some fun and then when we're done, both of them bitches are getting a bullet to the face."

Brian nodded in acknowledgment, then they sat on the cold, damp ground with their backs resting against a twisted, moss-encrusted oak tree and waited for darkness to fall.

11

Once night had fallen, the brothers refocused their attention on the tiny cottage, looking for any sign of their intended preys' whereabouts. "Look," Charles whispered to his brother pointing at the cottage as one of the windows illuminated brightly. "Let's go." The men pushed up from the ground and started to make their way towards the cottage but froze when they saw the front door open and someone emerge from inside.

"It's the daughter," Charles murmured as they watched Raven exit the home and make her way around towards the back of the property.

"New plan," Charles whispered to his bother. "Let's grab the young one first and we can use her as leverage to get the old bitch to do whatever the fuck we tell her to do."

***

"*What the hell is going on?*" Gwendolyn thought to herself as she continued her scrutiny of the scrying mirror and the mysterious black screen it continued to display. It was then that she noticed the screen wasn't entirely black as she had first assumed it to be. Upon closer inspection, she could ascertain that the reflection, however dark, showed shadows within shadows, which were moving. She suddenly realized that what she was actually seeing was the blackness of the bayou on a moonless night and that the darker shadows were the trunks of trees as one of the brothers moved through the dense bayou woodland.

"Now what are you boys up to? Gwendolyn asked aloud and then it hit her like a ton of bricks and she sprang up from the table with lightning speed and sprinted towards the front door.

12

Under the cover of darkness and assisted by the dense growth of trees and shrubbery in the area, Charles and Brian managed to creep, unnoticed, to within feet of Raven. "Now," Charles whispered as he and his brother sprinted out from behind a small cluster of trees. Raven's eyes went wide with shock when she saw the men running towards her, and before she knew it, they were on her. Charles slammed into Raven, full force, sending her tumbling to the ground and simultaneously knocking the wind out of her. Stunned by the suddenness of the attack, Raven shook her head in an attempt to clear the cobwebs and struggled to draw in a lung full of air as she tried to push herself up from the ground. She managed to croak out the smallest of screams before Charles was at her side, this time pulling a six-inch hunting knife from a hidden belt sheath and slamming her back to the ground, straddling her and pinning her arms to her side.

Just then, a voice rang out in the night. "Raven, where are you, girl?" Gwendolyn called as she exited the house and began to make her way towards the garden area.

Charles shot an irritated glance towards the home and pressed the tip of the blade to Raven's throat. "One word and I'll slit your fuckin' throat. Now, get up," he hissed, grabbing a handful of her locks. Raven let out a stifled yelp as Charles savagely yanked her to her feet and shoved her out of view against the trunk of a large cypress tree.

"Here, take her," Charles whispered

as he shoved Raven towards his brothe
along with his hunting knife. "Keep he
quiet." Brian whipped Raven around an
held her tight. One of his arms wrappe
around her waist, pinning her arms to he
side, and the other wrapped around he
neck, his hand placed over Raven's mouth
thus preventing her from alerting he
mother to her whereabouts. Charles
pulled his 9mm from the waistband of hi
pants and watched Gwendolyn who was diml
illuminated from the light shining
through the kitchen window as she
strolled cautiously towards the garden.

"Raven, stop playing around and come
inside immediately," Gwendolyn said
loudly, stopping midway between the house
and the garden. She stood silently and
tried to peer through the darkness in
search of her daughter but the night was
etched in charcoal and her vision failed
her mere feet from her location, not to
mention the sea of trees between herself
and the garden clearing which further
hindered her ability to locate her

missing offspring.

Irritated and starting to get a bit worried for the wellbeing of her daughter, Gwendolyn asked with a huff, "where the hell is she?" Charles watched from the concealment of the tree he stood behind as Gwendolyn walked towards to a large boulder that was covered in softly glowing lichen. Along the way, she stopped to pick up a two-foot-long branch that had fallen from the treetops overhead. When she reached the boulder, she pinched off a bit of the luminescent plant, rubbed it along the length of the stick, and chanted. *The night has awoken, with sleeping of sun. Concealing darkness be broken, light spell has begun.*

As she spoke the last word, the length of the stick she carried began to glow brightly, dispelling the darkness and illuminating everything within a twenty-foot radius from where Gwendolyn currently stood. Charles quickly ducked

out of sight and stood staring at hi
brother, wide-eyed and slack-jawed
"What the fuck?" he whispere
questioningly.

Brian stared back with the sam
astonished look on his face and whispere
in reply, "I fuckin' knew it, man.
fuckin' told you they were witches.
Both brothers stood in shocked silenc
trying to come to terms with the fac
that witches and witchcraft actuall:
exist and trying to discern their nex
move while taking into account this newl:
ascertained information.

Charles finally broke the silence
and said, "I don't give a fuck if these
bitches are related to Harry Fuckin'
Potter, both of them are gonna pay for
what they did to our friends." He then
stepped out from behind the tree and
called out to Gwendolyn. "Hey, witch,
looking for this?"

Gwendolyn's eyes went wide upon
seeing Charles step out from behind the

concealment of the tree and then instantly narrowed in anger when Brian came into view, toting Raven who was currently seized in a chokehold in front of him. Gwendolyn took notice of the gun Charles had pointed in her direction as well as the wicked-looking hunting knife Brian held to her daughter's abdomen. The tip of the blade was firmly pressed into the soft flesh, piercing her skin and beginning to stain her blouse a deep crimson.

"Son, you might want to take a minute to think about what you're getting yourself into," Gwendolyn calmly said. "If you know what's best, I suggest you have your brother release my daughter and then both be on your way, without any trouble."

Charles snorted then laughed. "Bitch, I don't know who the fuck you think you're talking to, but it don't look like either of you are in a position to be demanding shit," he responded.

"Now, what's gonna happen is you're gonn
walk over here, nice and easy, and don'
even think about trying to cast none o
your creepy ass voodoo magic on m
because you can rest assured that m
brother won't think twice about guttin
this bitch like a fish," he continued
pointing at Raven.

Gwendolyn cast a concerned look i
Raven's direction and raised her hands i
surrender. She knew she had to bide he
time and wait for just the right moment
to rectify their current situation. One
in which she could dispatch with both of
the men or at least incapacitate one or
the other enough to allow both she and
her daughter an opportunity to escape
this nasty state of affairs unscathed.
She briefly considered casting a Hold
Person spell, but in her haste to check
on the wellbeing of her daughter, she
left the house completely unprepared.
Though she knew the chant for the Hold
Person spell, she lacked a small straight
piece of iron—the required component

necessary to cast the spell. She silently scolded herself for making such a novice mistake and vowed never to do so again.

"Ok, ok…" Gwendolyn said, mock fear quivering her voice. "I give up. I'll do what you say, just promise not to hurt my daughter."

"Get moving," Charles said, inclining his head towards the house.

Gwendolyn's mind was running in circles, trying to conceive a suitable solution to their ill-fated predicament as she turned and began walking towards the house with Charles and Brian keeping a safe distance behind her, when suddenly, she recalled a rather basic but useful short-range teleportation incantation called Misty Step which required neither material nor somatic components. Simply speaking the words of the spell would ensure a successful casting. Now, all she had to do was think of a way to relay this information

to her daughter without alerting thei
wardens. Gwendolyn stopped just as sh
reached the front of the house—the ligh
from the front door, which was still ope
wide, illuminated the group. Gwendoly
slowly turned to face her captors an
smiled inwardly as she saw th
opportunity she was looking for. Rave.
was a few feet behind Charles, stil
being led by his brother who unknowingl
made the mistake of releasing his hol
over Raven's mouth and was now leadinς
her at arm's length with one hanc
gripping the back of her neck. Gwendolyr
locked eyes with her daughter and said ir
as casual a voice as she could muster,
"you guys should be cautious. The porch
tends to get a bit slippery and, Raven,
you know how much of a klutz you can be.
The night is misty, step carefully,
daughter."

Raven's eyes went bright with
understanding and she quietly whispered
the words for the Misty Step spell.
Instantaneously, a shimmering silvery

mist surrounded her, which caused Brian to let out a startled cry and prompted Charles to spin around to see what was happening. Raven vanished, then reappeared thirty feet away from the cottage and wasted no time darting off into the concealment of the nighttime bayou. Additionally, Gwendolyn seized the opportunity of Raven's disappearing act as she sprinted through the open front door when Charles turned his back to her, slamming the door closed and then throwing the lock in place behind her.

"Fuck," Charles exclaimed as the advantage he held over both Raven and Gwendolyn slipped through his fingers in a matter of seconds. "Don't just fucking stand there like an idiot, get after her," he scolded his brother.

Brian hesitated and stared into the darkness and finally said, "Bro, let's just get outta here. It's obvious we ain't dealing with no regular bitches. They're fuckin' witches, dude, no telling

what the hell they're capable of. I sa
we bounce and get as far away as possibl
as soon as possible."

"We're not going nowhere until bot
of these bitches are dead, you understan
me. Now stop actin' like a pussy and g
find the young one. We've seen them us
magic twice tonight. First, when the ol
one made the stick light up and just no
when the young one got away. The youn
one started whispering right before she
disappeared and earlier we heard the ol
hag rhyming right before the stick
started to glow. It's obvious that they
at least have to be able to speak to cast
their magic, so all you have to do is
find the daughter, sneak up on her, and
knock her the fuck out before she's able
to speak the words for any spell she
might try to hit you with." Charles
responded.

Though his brother's theory made
sense, Brian was still skeptical but he
nonetheless relented. "Fine, I doubt

she'd leave her mother so I'm sure she's still close by. I'll meet you back here when I have her," and with that, he turned and marched off into the bayou, following the same route the young witch had taken. Within seconds, he too was lost from sight as the darkness of the night enveloped him.

13

Once safely within the walls of her home, Gwendolyn stood with her back to the door and listened to the men's plan unfold. She heard the one called Brian as he stomped off the porch and went looking for Raven. Gwendolyn knew that Raven was familiar with the bayou surrounding the home like the back of her

hand, so she was secure in the knowledg
that Brian would not be able to locat
her daughter without significant effort
Just as Gwendolyn pushed off and made he
way toward the table upon which she lai
her accessories after returning home fro
her day's journey, thunderous jolt
rattled the door in its frame as Charle
tried to gain entry into the home b
kicking the door repeatedly. She quickl
slipped on the neckpiece along wit
several bracelets, then retrieved
costly-looking diamond and a putrid greer
foot-long tentacle which was sealed in
plastic bag from her artifact room, bot
of which she unceremoniously shoved int
a side pocket. She then hurriedly made
her way to the kitchen and glanced out
the window into the night. Gwendolyn
knew that her daughter was somewhere out
there and she needed her assistance to
finally be through with the annoyance
currently banging away at her front door.
She lifted her hand, fingered a helix
piercing of a tiny pair of linked silver

rings, and spoke the words for the Telepathy spell. *"Rings of silver, circled tight, carry word by day or night. Hear my words, hear my cries, across distance both far and wide."*

Raven could scarcely see the lights of her cottage through the trees as she stalked quietly through the bayou—sure she was being trailed by at least one, if not both of the men who had somehow managed to catch her and her mother unaware. She tried desperately to think of a useful spell that would somehow turn the tides to their advantage but, like her mother, Raven was ill-equipped and lacked the components necessary to cast anything beneficial. A subtle vibration of the piercing in Raven's upper ear alerted her to the fact that her mother was making an effort to communicate with her telepathically. She stopped, closed her eyes, and listened.

"Raven, can you hear me?" Gwendolyn asked, her voice reverberating through

her daughter's mind as if spoken throug
a long hollow tube.

"I'm here," Raven thought i
response. "Are you ok, mother?" concer
clearly evident in her thoughts whic
were, in turn, relayed to her mother.

"Not to worry, daughter, I'm fin
but I need you to return as quickly a
possible. The one known as Brian i
looking for you so be sure to stick t
the shadows and avoid detection. Make
your way to the rear of the house, the
other brother is still on the porch
kicking up quite a racket, trying t
break down the front door. I'm surprised
the poor dolt hasn't yet smashed the
window to gain entry but human men aren't
the brightest now, are they?" Gwendolyn
thought. "It's time we be done with this
game and I have the perfect culmination
of events in mind."

"I'm on my way now. It won't take
me long to return, I can see the light
shining through the kitchen window from

here," responded Raven before breaking the telepathic link to her mother and starting towards the house.

Gwendolyn ran over to her casting-cards, quickly flipped through them, and effortlessly located the spells she needed, thanks to the well-organized card catalogue system she had in place. She then made her way back to the kitchen window and peeked out, looking for any evidence of her daughter's whereabouts. Upon seeing her mother's silhouette appear in the small square of light, Raven stepped out from behind a nearby tree and waved. There was no back door as the home intentionally lacked any other ingress aside from the front door, for privacy and security reasons, so Gwendolyn quickly recited the words for the Misty Step spell and teleported outside. Raven ran up to her mother and hugged her tight. "Thank Goddess you're ok. I was so worried," she whispered quietly.

Payback is a Witch

Gwendolyn lovingly squeezed her bac and responded, "I was worried too daughter, but we've got to be swif before that ogre breaks down our fron door." She quickly removed a componen bracelet from her wrist and clamped i around her daughter's wrist. She the passed her a casting-card and continued "Quickly memorize this spell and be read to cast when I give the word." Rave glanced over the card and committed th spell to memory.

"What are we doing?" Raven asked curiously.

Gwendolyn smiled and replied, "you'll see, just follow my lead." With this, Gwendolyn waved the palm of her hand across her face as she quietly spoke the words for the Disguise-Self spell. Her image shimmered and altered into the spitting image of Brian. Raven smiled as she began to comprehend exactly what her mother had in mind. "Follow me," Gwendolyn said in Brian's voice, leading her daughter around the side of the house, and stopping midway between the back and front of the property. "Ok, now lay on the ground and close your eyes, as if you've been knocked out." Raven did as instructed then Brian took her by the wrist and dragged her the rest of the way towards the front of the house.

"Check it out, bro," Brian exclaimed triumphantly as he pulled Raven into view.

Charles swung his head to the left, a wicked grin splitting his face in two when he saw Raven at his brother's feet. "Bro, how the hell did you catch her so fast?"

Brian responded boastfully, "I saw the stupid bitch hiding in some bushes right behind the house so I picked up a big ass tree branch, snuck up on her, and fucked her up."

Charles smiled and turned his attention back to the door. "We got your

daughter, bitch, you hear me? You've go
ten seconds to open the fuckin' door an
bring yo ass out here before I star
carving this bitch like Hallowee
pumpkin," he shouted. He started bangin
away at the door when he noticed movemen
to the right in his peripheral vision
In one fluid movement, Charles spun t
his right and brought the gun he stil
held in his hand to bear on the figure
emerging from the darkness.

"Whoa, whoa, man, don't shoot. What
the fuck are you doing?" Brian asked,
throwing up his hands and taking a ste
back. Charles stared speechless, ther
swung his head back and forth from one
Brian to the other, his brow furrowed ir
confusion. Brian, upon seeing his
doppelganger standing over Raven at the
opposite end of the porch, took another
step back and let out an audible gasp.
"What the hell is going on?" he asked,
looking even more confused than his
brother did.

Payback is a Witch

The Brian looming over Raven, who was still lying on the ground feigning unconsciousness, shouted to Charles, "watch out, bro, it's her, it's the fuckin' witch. Shoot her, man," he urged, excitedly pointing in the direction of the real Brian.

Charles swung his head back to the solitary Brian and pointed the weapon in his direction. "Don't move or I swear I'll blow your damn head off."

Knowing that Charles was not above putting a bullet in his chest, Brian froze in place. "Come on, bro, it's me, your brother. She's fuckin' lying, don't listen to her," he said nervously.

"Oh yeah, if you're the real Brian, explain to me how I'm the one standing here with this bitch knocked out cold at my feet and not you." Fake Brian called out to the real Brian.

"Answer him," Charles shouted, his finger beginning to tighten on the trigger.

Gwendolyn saw her chance to put th
final nail in Brian's coffin and used i
to cast a low-level spell called Mino
Illusion, which required only a materia
component consisting of a small bit o
fleece and a minor somatic component—n
spoken incantation was needed. Charles'
back was turned towards her, hi
attention completely focused on th
solitary Brian so Gwendolyn lifted he
hands and drew the symbols required t
cast the Minor Illusion spell in the air
Upon completion, the most stereotypica
witches' cackle erupted from where the
real Brian was standing, which was al
the urging Charles needed. He pulled the
trigger, squeezing off two consecutive
rounds, both of which found their mark.
The first bullet hit Brian in the chest,
propelling him backwards, and the second
entered through his eye socket, exiting
the back of his skull in a spray of gore
and brain matter.

14

"Yes! We did it, bro," shouted Charles, turning away from the door and stepping off the porch. "Ding dong the mother-fuckin' witch is dead," he sing-songed.

With his attention diverted, Gwendolyn nudged Raven who had watched the scene unfold through hooded eyes. "Ok, daughter, hold him in place so we can be through with this nuisance, once and for all," she whispered.

Raven stood and recited the words for the Hold Person spell, speaking the last words just as Charles turned to face her. His eyes widened in shock and the hand still holding the 9mm began to rise—then everything froze. Though Charles was conscious and acutely aware of his predicament, he was completely

paralyzed—unable to move a singl
muscle. Unable to do anything to correc
the now obvious mistake in judgment h
made.

Brian, or at least the person he ha
assumed to be his true brother, walked u
to Charles, stood in front of him, an
with a dramatic flourish, dismissed th
Disguise Person spell. The illusio
dissipated and Charles stood face to fac
with the witch. So many emotions ra
through Charles's mind. Everything fro
disbelief to hate to despair, but th
emotion he felt more prominently than an
other was fear. However, the Hold Perso
spell made expressing any of the emotion
he was feeling unattainable.

Gwendolyn looked him in the eyes an
gently shook her head from side to side.
"Now, did you honestly believe you had a
chance in hell of besting us? Though I
do admit you did catch me off guard by
seeking us out. I never thought you had
it in you to be that presumptuous, a

valiant, yet fruitless effort on your part nevertheless."

Raven joined her mother, resting one arm on her shoulder and gave Charles a playful wink. "Remember me?" she asked mockingly. "All of this could have been avoided. Your brother and all of your foolish friends would still be alive if you would have gotten it through your thick skulls and understood that when a woman says no, she means no." Having spoken her piece, Raven stepped back to allow her mother room to carry out Charles's final sentencing.

Gwendolyn resumed her conversation with Charles. "Though your eventual fate will certainly be reminiscent to the friends who have gone before you, you should consider yourself privileged. You, my boy, will get to witness a place few are fortunate to behold and fewer still are able to venture into and live to speak of. Hell, my journey there to obtain a much sought-after component was

faced with peril and almost ended i
disaster, but I'm a crafty one
literally," she smiled at what sh
considered to be a very witty pun
"Still, I managed to escape none th
worse for wear with a highly sought-afte
Wiccan relic. Enough chit-chat, I'm sur
you're just dying to see what I'
prattling on about." With this
Gwendolyn stepped back and withdrew th
diamond she retrieved earlier from one o
the pockets concealed in the folds of he
skirt. She then spoke the words an
performed the somatic gestures require
for casting a high-level spell known a
Gate. *"Strange new world so far yet near,*
with these words shall now appear. A door
into shall open wide, and stay the
course, my will abide."

When the final word was spoken,
Gwendolyn quickly said to Raven, "look
away, daughter," she then tossed the
diamond on the ground a few feet in front
of Charles where it exploded with a
brilliant flash of pure white light.

Illuminating the night and bleaching the retinal pigment of Charles's eyes, causing temporary blindness as he was unable to shield his eyes from the blast. When the pigmentation in his eyes began to return to normal, so too did his vision. When his sight returned, in front of Charles floated a six-by-four-foot rift in the fabric of space and time and he stared into what he could only assume to be another dimension. It was utterly alien and unlike anything he had ever seen before.

The landscape rose and fell like placid waves on a massive ocean and glowed rosy hues of pink under a foreign sun, stretching out before him as far as his eyes could see. Not far in the distance, two bus-sized, insectoid-looking creatures with too many legs and wicked-looking pincers were in a ferocious battle for supremacy. The battle was short-lived as the weaker of the two fell before its brethren, bloodied and torn to shreds. The conqueror brutally ripped the head of his beaten opponent then scampered awa to enjoy the spoils of its victory leaving behind a trail of greenish-blu blood and gore in its wake. No soone than the creature departed, hordes o what looked to be foot-long iridescent colored flying squids emerged from withi massive earthen structures, resembling two-story-tall termite mound an overwhelmed the corpse, secretin yellowish, caustic mucus from anal gland upon landing, which caused the skin o the creature to begin to blister an dissolve. They then prodded th festering wound with a six-inch-lon proboscis, making a meal of the liquefie remains.

Before Charles could absorb any more detail of the nightmarish landscape, Gwendolyn stepped in front of him, peered through the threshold, and whispered in awe, "amazing, isn't it? Moreover, what you're seeing here is but merely the tip of the iceberg. There are specimens in this realm that defy the very imagination. Some are fantastical and wondrous while others are freakish and grotesque, the stuff born of nightmares." She turned away from the portal, faced Charles, reached within the folds of her skirt, and withdrew the plastic bag containing the tentacle. She removed the tentacle from the bag and wiggled it in front of Charles's face. "Why don't I introduce you to the latter of the two?" Gwendolyn taunted. As she began rubbing the slimy tentacle over Charles's extremities and face, he cringed inwardly. "This is a sliver of tentacle from the female of a species I suspect to be one of the realm's top apex predators which I managed to procure with maximum effort and at great peril to my wellbeing," she flung the feeler into the portal where it landed with a sickening splat. "Let's see if we can bait the male in for a closer look." She continued as both she and Raven retreated to a safe distance from the gateway, then waited.

For a while, nothing noteworth
happened as Charles continued hi
involuntary survey of the landscap
before him. His eyes riveted on th
corpse of the insectoid creature, fearfu
that one of the flying squids would los
interest in its meal, notice the strang
floating doorway, and decide to come an
investigate. He could image the thin
flying through the gateway, unloading
barrage of ass acid into his face, an
melting the skin off his skull i
preparation for consumption. Befor
long, a massive shadow fell across th
landscape followed by the tip of
tentacle, twice as long as Charles wa
tall, and as thick around as a two-liter
soda bottle, a dozen other appendages of
varying lengths and bulk immediately
joined it. The limbs swam through the
air languidly and snaked along the ground
gracefully, tasting and smelling their
surroundings with olfactory sensors
embedded within the end of each feeler.
One of the more slender arms located and

wrapped around the amputated piece of tentacle Gwendolyn tossed into the portal, then lifted it away and out of sight. Like a bloodhound on the scent of a rabbit, the mass of remaining tentacles turned and snaked towards and through the portal in the direction of Charles, one of the larger tentacles immediately wrapping around his leg.

"Release him," Gwendolyn instructed her daughter at which time Raven dismissed the Hold Person spell. The tentacle constricted and a sickening crunch of broken bones echoed through the night. Charles belted out a blood-curdling shriek of pain as he was snatched into the air and suspended seven feet above the ground, upside down by his left ankle. He somehow managed to retain his hold on the handgun and in a final, solitary act of defiance, he ground his teeth against the pain, took aim, and squeezed off a shot. The bullet found its mark, but his effort was pointless and ineffective as the creature barely

flinched. Another tentacle, however, di
shoot out from the writhing mass an
wrapped itself twice around Charles'
right arm, knocking the weapon from hi.
grasp. To his relief, the feeler did no
contract as he expected it to and brea
his arm as the other did his ankle, but
both appendages did very aggressivel;
twist and pull in opposite directions.
simultaneously wrenching his right arr
from its socket and separating his left
leg from its thigh. Charles screamec
like a banshee as his broken and manglec
body fell to the ground where it landec
with a wet staccato. He floundered about
on the soil like a fish out of water,
wailing in agony and bleeding profusely
from both ragged wounds. Thankfully, his
distress was short-lived as more
tentacles snaked around his body and
face. One wrapped around his head,
cutting off his anguished cries, then
squeezed, popping his skull like an
overripe melon. The feelers retreated
into the doorway, dragging the remains

with them as they did.

Gwendolyn and Raven stood transfixed as the brutal scene played out before them. Curious tentacles still explored the outer edge of the portal with more and more venturing further and further into our world. Both women recoiled when part of an eye filled the portal as the creature revealed more of itself while trying to venture a peek into the strange new land that had supplied it with a meager meal.

Though Gwendolyn knew there was no possible way the creature could gain entry into our universe via the small portal she opened, she also knew that the tentacles they had thus far witnessed were not a true indication of exactly how long and powerful the appendages truly were. If she did not close the doorway soon, the creature could do some serious damage to the surrounding bayou and to the home in which they lived. "Hurry, help me drag the body closer to the

gate," she said, inclining her hea
towards Brian's corpse. "Might as wel
use the beast to dispose of the boy'
remains," she continued grabbing one o
the boy's legs and pulling him close
with Raven's help. Within seconds,
feeler found and wrapped around Brian'
lifeless body, then effortlessly haule
it away.

Gwendolyn dismissed the portal wit
a flourish and it immediately began t
implode. The creature on the other side
sensed the gateway growing smaller and
smartly withdrew its appendages to avoid
amputation. Within seconds, the portal
vanished and the night was still.

"Well, that was the last of them,"
Raven said to her mother matter-of-
factly. "Do you think there's a chance
the police could track any of this back
to us?" she asked worriedly.

"It's doubtful," Gwendolyn responded
with conviction. "We were cautious with
the other men and as far as the final two

are concerned, with the lack of evidence, in particular, a body and with absolutely no witnesses, there is no way a prosecutor would have much of a case against us," she continued.

Raven looked anxiously at the remaining carnage of the night's events. Blood and gore-soaked much of the ground where Charles was dismembered, in addition to where Brian had been executed. She then looked to the 9mm handgun Charles abandoned upon his demise.

Gwendolyn took notice of the distressed look in her daughter's eyes and tried to reassure her, "Not to worry, a little effort and some resourceful use of the Prestidigitation spell will tidy this up without leaving a trace. As far as the weapon is concerned, we can dispose of it in one of the many waterways deep in the bayou where the resident alligators will no doubt preside over it with ferocious abandon." With this, Raven visibly relaxed a bit.

"I don't know about you but I'
still starving," Gwendolyn said, leadin
Raven into the cottage. "How about
finish warming the Gumbo and you run ou
to the garden to gather the lavender an
mint? We'll finish up with dinner an
then get some rest and maybe tomorrow w
can head into town to pick up som
supplies," she teased with a smirk and
sly wink.

"Ha-ha, very funny," Raver
responded, pursing her lips and cutting
her eyes at her mother as she exited the
room. The excitement and emotion of the
past few weeks caught up with Raven in
unison. She was suddenly exhausted and
looking forward to nothing more than a
hot bowl of spicy Louisiana Gumbo, a tall
glass of fresh lavender-mint tea, and a
good night's sleep.

ABOUT THE AUTHOR

Rowland Bercy Jr. author of Unbortion, winner of the 2020 American Fiction Awards, and finalist in the 2019 International Book Awards is originally from New Orleans, Louisiana and currently resides in Houston, TX.

BOOKS BY ROWLAND BERCY JR.
Unbortion
Pre-Thanksgiving Stress Disorder

ANTHOLOGIES
Homegrown Comeuppance / The Baker's Dozen
A Nec'ROMANTIC" Love Story / Battered, Broken Bodies
Pre-Thanksgiving Stress Disorder / The Distended Table

13322065R00081